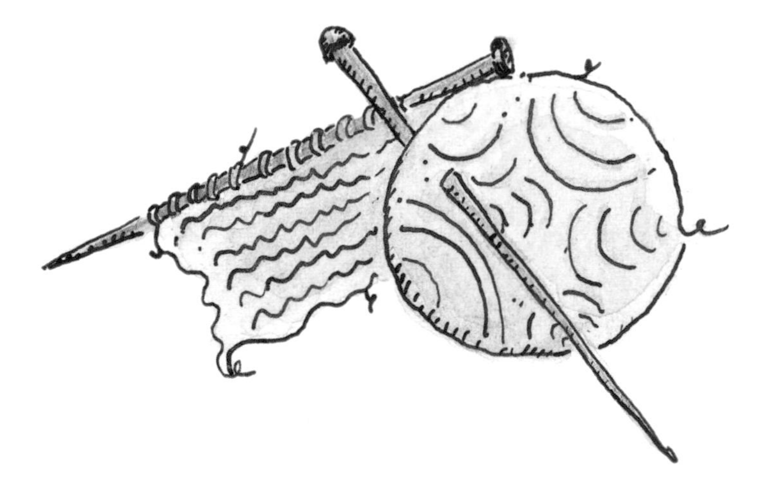

To my older brothers,
Paul and Dan,
who decided to keep me

Henry Holt and Company, LLC
Publishers since 1866
115 West 18th Street, New York, New York 10011
www.henryholt.com

Henry Holt is a registered trademark of Henry Holt and Company, LLC

Distributed in Canada by H. B. Fenn and Company Ltd.

Library of Congress Cataloging-in-Publication Data
Rubin, Vicky.
Ralphie and the swamp baby / Vicky Rubin.
Summary: Unhappy at the prospect of a new brother or sister joining his family, Ralphie,
a young alligator, sets out into the swamp in search of a stork to whom he can return the egg.
[1. Babies—Fiction. 2. Brothers and sisters—Fiction. 3. Alligators—Fiction.
4. Storks—Fiction. 5. Swamps—Fiction.] I. Title.
PZ7.R831326Ral 2004 [E]—dc21 2003007065

ISBN 0-8050-6836-8 / EAN 978-0-8050-6836-8 / First Edition—2004 / Designed by Donna Mark
Printed in the United States of America on acid-free paper. ∞

10 9 8 7 6 5 4 3 2 1

The artist used pen and ink, watercolor, colored pencil, and crayon
on Fabriano paper to make the illustrations in this book.

Ralphie and the Swamp Baby

Vicky Rubin

Henry Holt and Company • New York

SCHOOL

Ralphie hurried home from school, happily clutching his mud-wrestling trophy. Mom and Dad would be so proud!

“Look what I won!” he shouted. But Dad went on humming a lullaby, and Mom barely looked up from her knitting. Why was she making such a tiny sweater?

Mom smiled. “Ralphie,” she said, “we’re going to hatch an egg. Come see—but be very careful!”

An EGG!

Ralphie looked at the smooth, shiny egg. Then he looked at his own scaly green skin. He turned emerald with envy.

The egg got lots of attention. Everyone read to it, sang to it, and decorated its room. It even got phone calls.

Grandma Saurus couldn't stop talking about the you-know-what.

“Grandma, do you want to hear a joke?” Ralphie asked as he helped her pickle minnows.

“Certainly,” she said. “You know I love yolks!”

The next week Ralphie won a crayfish-catching trophy, but his family barely seemed to care. They were too busy admiring the egg. He had to get rid of it. But how?

“What kind of baby has the stork brought from the swamp?” Grandma Saurus wondered. “A boy or a girl?”

Of course! Ralphie could give the egg back to the stork!

That night, after everyone was asleep, Ralphie stared at the silent egg. "You are in my power now," he whispered as he snatched it up and headed for the swamp.

When Ralphie got there he asked an elderly turtle where the stork lived.

"Up in that tree," the turtle said, eyeing the egg curiously.

Ralphie took a deep breath.
"There's nothing to be afraid of,"
he told himself and climbed
up the slippery trunk.

"Careful, now!"
called the turtle.

Ralphie looked for the stork's nest.

Oh, no! It was far below him, on the other side of the tree.

He heard a strange noise. "What . . . who . . . ?" he whispered and glanced around nervously.

KNOCK KNOCK. It was coming from the egg!

Ralphie gasped. That was his brother or sister knocking! What would the baby be like? If he gave the egg back to the stork he'd never know. Was it too late to change his mind?

Suddenly a giant shape loomed over him.

“Get away from there, you big lizard!” it screamed. The stork!

Ralphie was so surprised he dropped the egg. “No!” he cried and dove after it.

He caught it right before he bellyflopped into the nest.

The stork whisked her own eggs to a safe branch and glared at Ralphie.

He gulped and asked politely, “Is this yours?”

“Nest-wrecker!” she hissed.

“I am not!” Ralphie protested. “I was only trying to return your egg, but now I’ve decided to keep it.”

The stork laughed until tears ran down her bill. "*My* egg? You b-believed that old alligator story?"

"I don't see what's so funny," Ralphie said. "Didn't you bring this egg to my mom?"

“Young reptile,” the stork said, “storks lay stork eggs, alligators lay alligator eggs, and flies lay fly eggs. And that’s that.” She picked him up in her talons.

“What about bears?” Ralphie asked.

“Bears are another story,” she said firmly and set him down on the ground.

Ralphie heard frantic voices calling across the swamp.

“My egg!” Mom cried.

“My son!” Dad yelled.

“My goodness!” Grandma Saurus exclaimed as Ralphie ran toward them.

They hugged Ralphie and tickled his belly and took him home for a wonderful breakfast of poached tadpoles.

Then Mom reached into her knitting pouch. "Look, I made matching sweaters for you and the baby!"

Ralphie smiled.

"So tell us," said Dad. "What were you doing in the swamp?"

"I was . . . I was . . ." The stork had laughed when Ralphie told her about the egg. What if his family laughed too?

Grandma Saurus winked at Ralphie and grasped his claw under the table.

"Listen!" she said. "Do you hear something?" Everyone rushed over to the egg.

KNOCK KNOCK . . .

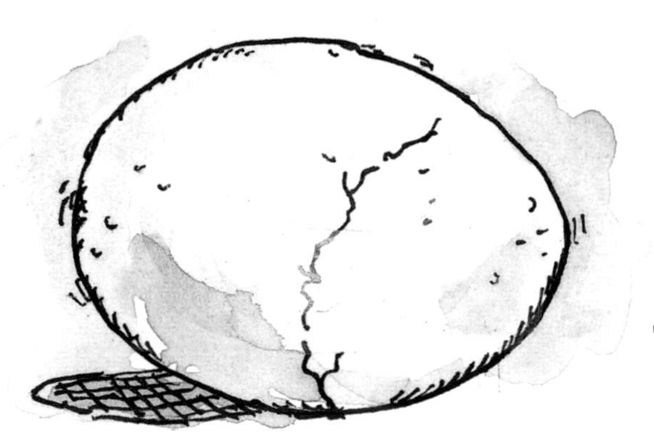

Then came a faint cracking noise.

It grew louder . . .

and louder . . .

"It's a girl!" Dad shouted.

"My little swamp baby!" Mom cried.

Ralphie looked at his new baby sister. He was awfully glad he'd decided to keep her!

The alligators cheered.

Ralphie cheered loudest of all.